Night Walk

Story by Jill Newsome

Illustrations by Claudio Muñoz

Clarion Books • New York

To Liliana –
and to all dog and cat lovers

Clarion Books
a Houghton Mifflin Company imprint • 215 Park Avenue South, New York, NY 10003
Text copyright © 2002 by Jill Newsome • Illustrations copyright © 2002 by Claudio Muñoz

First published in Great Britain in 2002 by Andersen Press, Ltd., 20 Vauxhall Bridge Road, London SW1V 2SA.
Published in the United States in 2003.

www.houghtonmifflinbooks.com

Printed in Italy.

Library of Congress Cataloging-in-Publication Data
Newsome, Jill. • Night walk / story by Jill Newsome ; illustrations by Claudio Muñoz.
p. cm.
Summary: When Daisy, an adventurous dog, persuades Flute, a stay-at-home cat, to go for a walk one night, Flute gets more than she bargained for.
ISBN 0-618-32458-5 (alk. paper) • [1. Dogs—Fiction. 2. Cats—Fiction.] I. Muñoz, Claudio, ill. II. Title.
PZ7.N48664 Ni 2003 • [E]—dc21   2002010266
10 9 8 7 6 5 4 3 2 1

Outside in the garden,
the blackbird sings
her morning song.
Flute the cat and
Daisy the dog
wake up.

Daisy rushes wildly upstairs.
Flute just stretches and yawns.

Daisy has breakfast . . .

. . . then goes for a walk.

Flute waits till Daisy is out
and the house is quiet.

Now she has breakfast . . .

. . . and a stroll in the garden.

But soon Daisy is home again.

"You smell different," Flute says to Daisy. "Where have you been?"
"To the park," answers Daisy. "With the rabbits and the squirrels."
"What are rabbits and squirrels?" asks Flute.
"Well . . ." says Daisy, "a rabbit is like a giant mouse with very long ears, and a squirrel is a sort of rat with a fluffy tail who lives up in a tree."

"Really?" says Flute.
She's curious. She has never
seen animals like that.

This evening the moon is shining and Daisy is going for a night walk.
Flute has never been beyond the garden gate, but she does love the night.

She thinks she might go along.

Bravely stepping out,
she follows Daisy up the road.

"Oh, good!" says Daisy. "We'll go to the park together!" Flute wonders what the park is like.

The night is full of strange
smells, strange noises,
and, worst of all . . .

But Daisy
is there in an instant
to frighten them all away.

Staying close together, they
reach the gates of the park.
It's an enormous wild place.
"Oh, dear!" says Flute.

Daisy dashes off, chasing
a shadow into the night.
Flute rushes up
the nearest tree.

Two large eyes
peer out of the dark.
"Good evening!" says a voice.
"And what can I do for you?"
"Oh, dear!" says Flute.

She dives into the bushes below.
"Hello," says a voice. "We don't
know you. Who are you?"
"Oh, dear!" says Flute.

Just then there's a screech from above. "Help! There's trouble ahead! Follow me!" The strange animals start running, and Flute finds herself running with them. Suddenly she sees . . .

A huge wild cat has taken Daisy prisoner!
"Oh, no!" says Flute.

Hissing and spitting, Flute charges forward.
"Hey, you big brute!" she shrieks. "Leave my friend alone!"

"Flute!" gasps Daisy.
The other animals surround the wild cat.

"Your friend came too close," she growls.
"I'm protecting my babies." Sure enough, four
little faces are peeking through the brambles.
"I'm sorry," says Daisy. "I only wanted to play."

So one by one the kittens come out and play with Daisy.

Soon it's time to go home.

"You were so brave!" says Daisy. "What would I have done without you?" Flute just smiles.

"You'll come along next time, won't you?" says Daisy.

"No, thank you," says Flute.

Adventure may be exciting once in a while,
but a quiet house is better.

Sleep well, Daisy!
Sweet dreams, Flute!